TRIXIE &JINX

Dean Koontz

ILLUSTRATED BY Janet Cleland

G. P. Putnam's Sons • An Imprint of Penguin Group (USA) Inc.

G. P. PUTNAM'S SONS

A division of Penguin Young Readers Group.

Published by The Penguin Group. Penguin Group (USA) Inc., 375 Hudson Street, New York, NY 10014, U.S.A. Penguin Group (Canada), 90 Eglinton Avenue East, Suite 700, Toronto, Ontario M4P 2Y3, Canada (a division of Pearson Penguin Canada Inc.). Penguin Books Ltd, 80 Strand, London WC2R ORL, England. Penguin Ireland, 25 St. Stephen's Green, Dublin 2, Ireland (a division of Penguin Books Ltd.). Penguin Group (Australia), 250 Camberwell Road, Camberwell, Victoria 3124, Australia (a division of Pearson Australia Group Pty Ltd). Penguin Books India Pvt Ltd, 11 Community Centre, Panchsheel Park, New Delhi - 110 017, India. Penguin Group (NZ), 67 Apollo Drive, Rosedale, North Shore 0632, New Zealand (a division of Pearson New Zealand Ltd). Penguin Books (South Africa) (Pty) Ltd, 24 Sturdee Avenue, Rosebank, Johannesburg 2196, South Africa. Penguin Books Ltd, Registered Offices: 80 Strand, London WC2R ORL, England.

Design by Richard Amari.

Text set in Gothic Blond Husky.

The art was done in watercolor and pen and ink.

Library of Congress Cataloging-in-Publication Data

Koontz, Dean R. (Dean Ray), 1945– Trixie and Jinx / Dean Koontz ; illustrated by Janet Cleland. p. cm. Summary: Golden retriever Trixie misses her best friend, wiener dog Jinx, when Jinx's family takes him on vacation. [1. Stories in rhyme. 2. Best friends—Fiction. 3. Friendship—Fiction. 4. Golden retriever—Fiction. 5. Dachshunds—Fiction. 6. Dogs—Fiction.] I. Cleland, Janet, ill. II. Title. PZ8.3.K842Tri 2010 [E]—dc22 2009034957

ISBN 978-0-399-25197-9

1 3 5 7 9 10 8 6 4 2

To Gerda,
　　　with love and puppy love.
　　　　　　　　D.K.

For Jim,
　　　my wonderful husband
　　　　　and constant companion.
　　I could never have gone down this road
　　　　　without you.
　　　　　　　J.C.

I, Trixie,
am having fun summer . . .

. . . stalking
what slinks,

sniffing
what stinks,

running and chasing with
   my best friend, Jinx.

We play video games when his
family's out for the day.

We read books in the nook when my family's away.
Jinx is the best that a best friend can be.

But suddenly summer turns dark, turns bleak.
Jinx and his folks are going away for a week.

A week is forever.
  Don't you know,
    dinosaurs walked the earth a week ago?

Jinx and his family are leaving with surfboards,
with beach balls, with sunglasses, oh gee . . .

. . . without me.

Without a friend,
    there's so much you can't do.

Seesaw.

Rickshaw.

Ping-pong.

Old Maids.

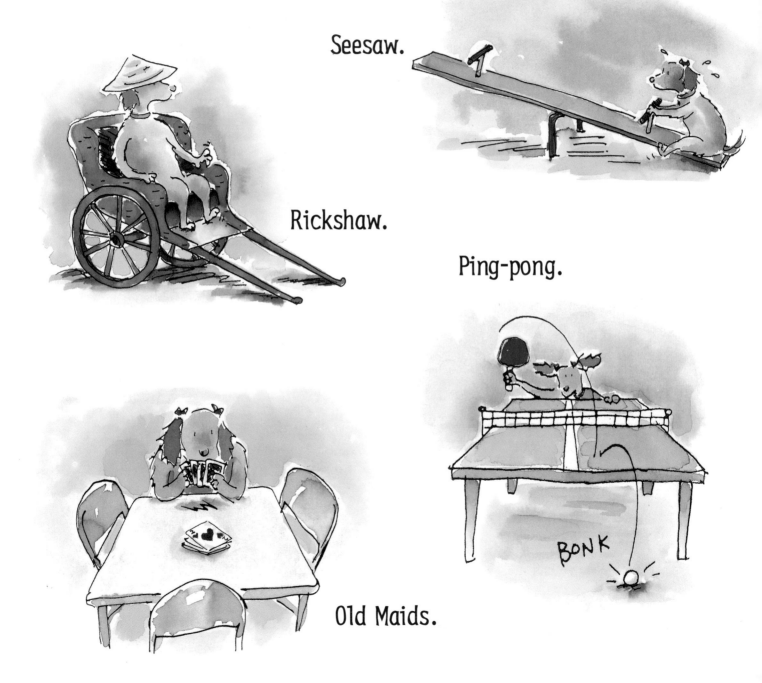

Charades.

Discuss literature.

Share an éclair. . .

(Okay, almost never,
    but sometimes, you see,
        being alone is a good
            thing to be.)

Eating an éclair
    takes half of a half of one minute or so.
      Then what?
        What's to do?
          Where to go?
            Don't know.

Me and Jinx are the only dogs on our street.
But maybe there's some new friend I can meet.
The boy next door—
his pet has eight feet.

I tell it my best joke about cats.
No chuckle, no giggle, no laugh, no curtain call.
Things that eat flies have no humor at all.

There's a mouse in the house.
Be my friend, please?
We have so much in common—
a love of good cheese.

After cheese, what we have in common is tails.

I chase mine, chase, chase, chase.

But mousey refuses to chase his own.

I chase mine, I chase mine, around and around.

He goes home.

To be dog's best friend . . .

Ants are too small.

Giraffes are too tall.

Bees are too stingy.

Snakes are too thingy.

I, Trixie, who is dog,
   will have the best kind of best friend who ever could be,
      one who is entirely imaginary!
         I'll call her Dixie. And she will be,
            oh, she will be, furry and fun
               'cause she'll be just like me!

Dixie, do you want tea?

Well, Trixie, do You want tea?

Yes, I want tea.

Then, I want tea too.

If Jinx were here, we could search the woods,
paw beside paw,
maybe find a dinosaur bone to gnaw.

Or we could practice our balancing act.
We've got good balance, and that's a fact.

Jinx is just a wiener dog,
smaller than tall,
can't swim at all,
longer than strong,
but each day without him
is dull and so wrong.

But wait!
I smell the smell of a wiener dog I know very well!
In flip-flops, baggies, sunglasses and hair gel,
the beach hound is home with stories to tell.

Stories of sharks and pirates
and whales.
Jinx is not nearly as tall
as his tales.

But a friend always listens and laughs when she should,
and says her friend's stories are wonderfully good.
And I'm sure you don't have to be told
that a friend is more precious than pirate gold.